FRED

Picture books by Posy Simmonds in Red Fox

FRED

F-FREEZING ABC

BOUNCING BUFFALO

In memory of R.H.J.

A Red Fox Book

Published by Random House Children's Books
20 Vauxhall Bridge Road, London SW1V 2SA

A division of Random House UK Ltd
London Melbourne Sydney Auckland
Johannesburg and agencies throughout the world

Copyright © Posy Simmonds 1987

1 3 5 7 9 10 8 6 4 2

First published in Great Britain by Jonathan Cape Limited 1987
Red Fox edition 1998

Printed in Singapore

RANDOM HOUSE UK Limited Reg. No. 954009

ISBN 0 09 926412 9

FRED

POSY SIMMONDS

RED FOX

Sophie and Nick sit on the step outside their house feeling sad....

Everyone is sad when they hear the news....

Fred used to sleep *all* the time.

He also liked eating....

...and purring and sitting on laps...

...but, most of all, he liked sleeping....

...on the ironing board...

...on the washing...

...on top of the fridge.....

....in patches of sunlight....

...and, especially, on beds.

Now Fred is buried at the end of the garden, underneath the buddleia....

Nearby are the graves of a guinea pig and a beetle, which Sophie marked with stones....

He was the laziest cat in the world, Fred was...

Fat old Fred

Zat what you're putting on his gravestone?

No, dumbo! You have to write something *nice!*

I dunno what to put....

I'll just write his name ...*stop* jogging me!

There...

Fred

O poor, poor Fred!

Poor Fred is dead!

The most FAMOUS cat in the WORLD!

But WHY was he FAMOUS? .... WHY?

Kindly lower your voice!

But he just SLEPT all day!!

He slept all day... but...at NIGHT..?

At night, Mum put him out...

Yes! And every night, HOW we waited for that moment....

...when the back door would open......

Out you go, Fred... Night, night

...and the lights went out, and all was hushed.....

...and then, Fred would make his bow....

...and start to sing...

MeYOWL!

Fred SANG?!!

.O Caterwauley-wailey-woe...O Woe, O woe weeooo!

Then, one by one, the mourners lay their wreaths and flowers on the grave.

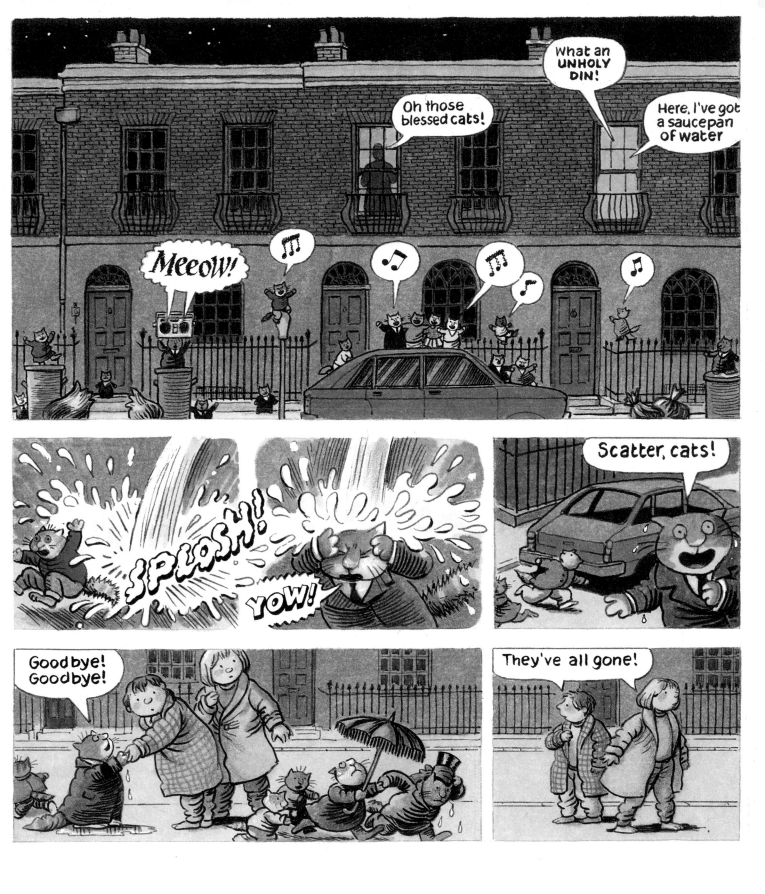

Sophie and Nick creep in through the front door....

....tiptoe up the stairs.......and climb into bed.....

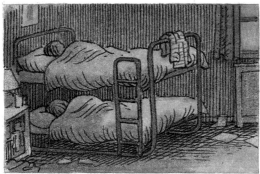

...and soon, first Nick....and then Sophie, fall fast asleep.

It's *funny* the next morning.....

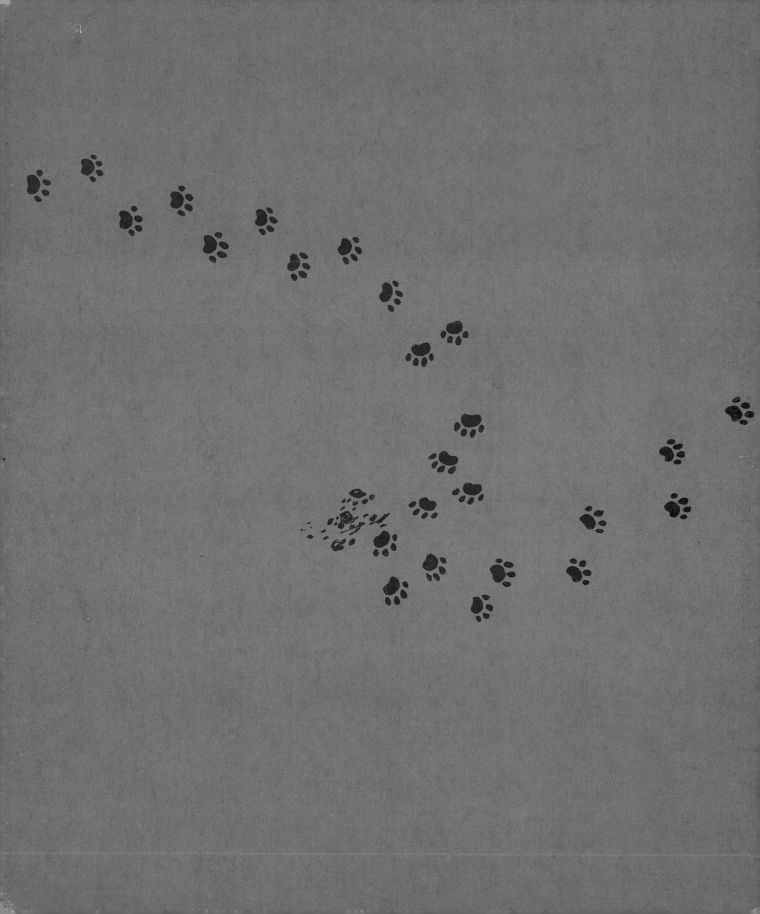

Some bestselling Red Fox picture books

THE BIG ALFIE AND ANNIE ROSE STORYBOOK
by Shirley Hughes
OLD BEAR
by Jane Hissey
OI! GET OFF OUR TRAIN
by John Burningham
DON'T DO THAT!
by Tony Ross
NOT NOW, BERNARD
by David McKee
ALL JOIN IN
by Quentin Blake
THE WHALES' SONG
by Gary Blythe and Dyan Sheldon
JESUS' CHRISTMAS PARTY
by Nicholas Allan
THE PATCHWORK CAT
by Nicola Bayley and William Mayne
WILLY AND HUGH
by Anthony Browne
THE WINTER HEDGEHOG
by Ann and Reg Cartwright
A DARK, DARK TALE
by Ruth Brown
HARRY, THE DIRTY DOG
by Gene Zion and Margaret Bloy Graham
DR XARGLE'S BOOK OF EARTHLETS
by Jeanne Willis and Tony Ross
WHERE'S THE BABY?
by Pat Hutchins